How to Handle a Bully

a Bully

by
Nancy Wilcox Richards

illustrations by
David Sourwine

SCHOLASTIC INC.
New York Toronto London Auckland
Sydney Mexico City New Delhi Hong Kong

ISBN 978-0-545-28309-0

12 11 10 9 8 7 6 5 4 3 2 1   11 12 13 14 15/0

Printed in the U.S.A.   40

First Scholastic Book Clubs printing, October 2010

For Mom, who shared her own stories about being bullied, and for Dad, who worked a second job to buy me my very first two-wheeler.

— N.W.R.

Chapter 1

My name is Marilla — but everyone calls me Rilla for short. Right now I'm in Grade Three. But in two more months it'll be summer vacation. Then it's on to Grade Four. I'm kind of excited and a little bit nervous about Grade Four.

The good things about Grade Three include Ms MacArthur — she's everybody's favorite teacher — plus there's no homework on the weekends. And I really like being with my friends Tony, Lauren and Nicholas. The bad things about Grade Three include super hard math and playground cleanup duty. It is totally gross picking up slimy garbage.

Grade Four will be hard. I know there will be a lot more homework. And what if none of my friends are in the same class? But the worst thing is Mr. Dean. The kids call him Mr. Mean because when he yells, the whole school can hear him. He gives tons of detentions. I sure hope I'm not in his class.

Right now, Ms MacArthur is getting ready to have our usual Morning Meeting. She tells us important stuff — like if we have music or gym. Sometimes she tells us about a new school rule. Lots of mornings she starts off with a riddle. That's my favorite part.

"Good morning, everyone!" Ms MacArthur smiled. Then she paused and looked toward the side of the room. "I'll wait just another moment until Bethany joins us for the meeting." Twenty-two pairs of eyes turned to watch Bethany stuff something in her desk and then scurry over to sit on the mat. "Now," continued Ms MacArthur, "the biggest news of the day is this." She waved a sheet of paper. "A fitness challenge will take place next month at the community park."

"Cool!" yelled Nicholas.

"What do we have to do?" asked Lauren.

Ms MacArthur held up her hand for quiet. "Let me read this to you." She unfolded the paper. "Come to Bayfield Community Park and join us for some fun and challenging activities at the First Annual Bayfield Fitness Challenge. Test your strength by doing chin-ups. Race through the tire run. Try your luck on the bicycle obstacle course. And much, much more! Earn points and you could win a brand new X-Treme bike, complete with a water bottle and matching helmet."

"Sweet!" said Tony.

Ms MacArthur pinned the poster on the bulletin board. "You can check out all the details here," she said. "Now, I have just a few reminders for you boys and girls. First, it's a gym day, and second, Vanessa Cardui will be joining our class tomorrow. I think you'll all really enjoy having Vanessa in our class."

"Who's she?" asked Lauren. "Can she sit by me?"

Ms MacArthur laughed. "Patience, patience. You'll meet Vanessa Cardui tomorrow. But before we head back to our groups to finish yesterday's art project, I have a little riddle to start our day. Ready?"

Most of us nodded our heads. This was my favorite part of the Morning Meeting.

"What do you call a funny book about eggs?"

I glanced around. Everyone was thinking really hard. Eyes scrunched. Heads tilted.

"What do you call a funny book about eggs?" I repeated. "I know! I know!" I shouted.

Ms MacArthur smiled at me. "Rilla, what do you call a funny book about eggs?"

"A *yolk* book!" and I laughed.

There were a few groans in the room.

"Good one," said Claire. She usually guesses the riddles before anyone else. "I'll have to try that one on my dad tonight."

Then Ms MacArthur clapped her hands. "Okay, kids. Back to your groups. We need to finish that art project today."

"Hey, Rilla," Tony whispered to me from his seat, "are you going to enter the fitness challenge? *I* definitely am. I'm in pretty good shape from hockey." He flexed a muscle and then laughed.

"Me, too!" answered Lauren. "The park is right across the street from my house. I go there every day. I can practice on the playground equipment whenever I want."

I looked down at my sneakers and scuffed my toe across the floor. "Not sure," I mumbled.

"You should," coaxed Nicholas. "No one can beat you when we do chin-ups in gym. And I've watched you on the monkey bars. You're really fast."

I could feel everyone looking at me. Waiting for an answer. My face was warm. "Um . . ." I paused, and whispered, "I don't know how to ride a two-wheeler. I still use training wheels."

"Oh," said Nicholas, and he sounded just about as sad as I did.

Chapter 2

The next morning Ms MacArthur said, "Class, today you'll meet Vanessa Cardui."

I looked around. So did everyone else. I didn't see the new girl anywhere.

"I wonder when she'll get here?" whispered Lauren.

I shrugged my shoulders. I kind of hoped she could sit at my table. I waved my hand in the air. "Ms MacArthur! Ms MacArthur! Can Vanessa sit with me?"

Ms MacArthur laughed. "Actually, Rilla, Vanessa will sit with all of you."

Now that did *not* make sense. There was no way she could sit at six different tables. But before I could ask any questions, there was a knock at the door. Maybe it was her.

"Ah." Ms MacArthur beamed. "Vanessa Cardui is finally here."

I looked for the new girl. But all I saw was the secretary. She handed the teacher a large box. Where was Vanessa?

"Can you see her?" Nicholas asked me.

"Nope."

"Hey, Tony!" whispered Nicholas. "Can you see the new girl?"

Tony shook his head.

Then Ms MacArthur held up the box. "Here is Vanessa."

I looked at Nicholas. He shrugged his shoulders. This was weird. There was no way a kid could be in a box.

"Now," began Ms MacArthur, "I can see you're all puzzled. I guess this is a bit like another one of my riddles." She paused to make sure she had everyone's attention. "*Vanessa cardui* isn't actually a person. 'She,' or I guess I should say 'it,' is in the box. Anybody want to guess what *Vanessa cardui* might be?"

Huh? Vanessa wasn't a new girl? I thought about what it could be. Before I could guess, Bethany called out from the back of the room.

"Is it a gerbil?"

Ms MacArthur shook her head.

"Is it a rabbit?" guessed Tony.

Again, Ms MacArthur shook her head.

"I know!" yelled Lauren. "Vanessa is a hedgehog!"

Everyone laughed, including the teacher.

"Here's a riddle to help solve the mystery.

Ready?" Ms MacArthur wrote on the board:

> I have more than four legs.
>
> My baby does not look like me.
>
> I taste with my feet.
>
> What am I?

I was pretty sure that the first clue meant it had to be an insect. But what animal tastes with its feet?

Hands went up around the room.

"Is it a grasshopper?" guessed Aaron.

Ms MacArthur shook her head.

"Is it a spider?" guessed James.

Ms MacArthur shook her head.

"Is it an octopus?" guessed Claire.

Again Ms MacArthur shook her head. "Here it is," she said, and she pulled a jar out of the box. It looked like it was filled with leaves. "These thistle leaves are covered with tiny eggs," she explained. "Over the next few days they will hatch into . . ."

"Caterpillars!" I shouted.

Ms MacArthur smiled at me. "That's right, Rilla. And then eventually the caterpillars will become butterflies — Painted Lady butterflies, to be exact. Or as scientists like to call them, *Vanessa cardui*."

So now we knew. *Vanessa cardui* wasn't a new girl. It was our latest science project.

Chapter 3

The eggs were really tiny. They were only as big as the head of a pin. By the end of the day, some of the eggs had already hatched. Now, I usually think of caterpillars as cute and furry. But these things were ugly. They reminded me of grey worms with just a few hairs. Kind of gross. Ms MacArthur gave us each a little jar with some thistle leaves. And the best part was that everybody got some eggs or a few caterpillars.

"Boys and girls, before you get on the bus, label your jars and put your larvae on the back counter."

So now we have a whole pile of jars filled with leaves and caterpillars — or larvae, as Ms MacArthur calls them.

Everyone headed out to the hall. Nicholas and Lauren were putting on their jackets.

"I'll meet you at the park in half an hour," Nicholas said to Lauren.

"Great!" she answered. "We'll be able to do lots of practicing for the Fitness Challenge." She looked over at me. "Hey, Rilla! You going to the park?"

"Um," I mumbled, "I'm not sure."

"Pleeease," begged Lauren. "It'll be lots of fun."

"We can do the tire run," added Nicholas. "I need lots of work on that. Bet I can beat you." He grinned at me.

Part of me wanted to go. Another part didn't. "Okay," I agreed reluctantly. "I'll meet you at the park."

* * *

I was surprised to see James, Aaron and Claire there when I arrived. It seemed like we all had the same idea. Everyone wanted that new bike. James was swinging across the monkey bars. Aaron was trying to do a few chin-ups. But I think he was finding it pretty hard. Claire was crawling as fast as she could through a big tube. Everything looked like so much fun.

"Hi, Rilla! You're early," came a voice from across the park.

I turned to see Nicholas and Lauren ride their bikes through the gate.

"Let's get started!" shouted Nicholas. "Race you to the monkey bars!"

We were having a blast when Lauren nudged me. "Look over there," she said. She pointed to some kids coming through the gate.

There were only three of them. But one was really big — and they all looked mean. And the bad thing was, they were heading our way.

I gulped. "Who are they?" I asked Lauren. But before she could answer, the big kid came right over to us. "We're here to use the equipment," he snarled. "So beat it."

"W-w-what?" I stammered.

"You deaf or something? I *said*, me and the other River Rats are here to use this stuff." He pointed to the equipment. Then he pointed at Aaron. "Hey, Oliver, check this out. That baby can't even do a chin-up."

I glanced over at Aaron. His face was red and he looked ready to cry. So now I knew one of the kids' names — Oliver. And River Rats? What was that? A gang?

Lauren spoke first. Her voice sounded quivery. "We were just leaving." She looked at the Bayfield kids. "Let's go."

You didn't need to tell me twice to get out of there. My heart was pounding. My mouth was dry. My hair felt like it was standing on end. Once we were outside the park, I stole a backward glance. The River Rats were climbing on the jungle gym. "Do you know them?" I asked Lauren.

She shook her head. "Not really. They were in baseball last summer. They call themselves the River Rats. They're from Riverdale School. Cameron's the big one and the twins are Oliver and Olivia. They do everything he tells them to do." She paused for a minute like she was remembering something. She frowned. "I'm pretty sure they don't live around here. I live right over there," Lauren pointed to a grey house across the street, "and I've never seen them at the park before. They probably won't be back." She looked at me and the other Bayfield kids. "Let's come back tomorrow."

I glanced at Aaron, James and Nicholas. I knew what they were thinking, just by looking at their faces. They didn't want to come back. Neither did I. But I was too chicken to say so.

"Okay," I said slowly. "We'll try it again after school tomorrow."

Chapter 4

The next day, as soon as I got to school I checked my eggs. Almost all of them had hatched. Some caterpillars were crawling on the sides of the jars. The rest were eating leaves. They looked a lot bigger.

"They're growing fast, aren't they?" remarked Ms MacArthur. She knelt down beside me, peering into the jar.

I nodded my head. "But some of them aren't moving," I said.

Ms MacArthur took a closer look. "It seems as though a few have died."

"Already?" I asked.

The teacher nodded her head. "It's the way nature works. If all the insects that hatched lived, the world would be overrun with them."

She patted my arm. "Don't worry, Rilla. We'll have plenty of caterpillars."

Nicholas came over to look at his caterpillars. "Hey, cool!" he shouted. "Check this out. All my eggs have hatched!"

James, Lauren and Claire raced over.

"Mine, too!"

"Same here!"

"Okay, class, let's put the larvae back on the counter. It's time for our Morning Meeting," announced Ms MacArthur. "Please come back to the story carpet."

Lauren tugged on my sleeve as we went to the back of the room. "Do you want to go to the park on Saturday? We can do some more practicing."

"Sure," I paused. "Do you think the River Rats will be there again?"

"I don't think so," she answered.

I felt a bit better. I definitely didn't want to go to the park if those bullies were there.

"And bring your bike this time," added Lauren. "We can practice the obstacle course."

There it was again. It all came back to the bike and the obstacle course. How was I going to compete using training wheels? Everyone would laugh at me. Training wheels were for babies. Only a loser would use them. "Um," I said, and I didn't look Lauren in the eye, "I don't know if I can make it."

"Is this about the training wheels?" asked Lauren. "Because if it is, Nicholas and I will help you. It'll be easy. You'll see."

I wasn't so sure about that. I had already tried to ride my big brother's bike a few

times. It always ended in disaster. Bloody
knees. Bloody elbows. And the last time, a
loose tooth.

We sat down on the mat and Ms MacArthur
began talking about the things we would do
that day. At the end of the meeting she held
up some stapled booklets. "Today each of you
will receive a Life Cycle Journal. I'd like you
to write in it every day. Record any changes
that you see in your larvae. You might like
to draw some pictures as well." She smiled.

"Now, before we start our journals, I have a new riddle for you."

I inched a little closer.

"Where would you put an injured insect?"

I couldn't think of an answer but, as usual, Claire was waving her hand in the air. So was James.

"James?" asked Ms MacArthur.

"In the hospital," he guessed.

Ms MacArthur shook her head. "Anyone else want to make a guess?" She looked at Claire and repeated the question, "Where would you put an injured insect?"

"That's an easy one," answered Claire. "In the *ant*-bulance." And she laughed out loud.

The teacher laughed, too. "It's so hard to stump you, Claire. I think you should ask us a riddle on Monday."

"Sure," Claire replied. She looked really happy. "But it'll be a tricky one."

After that, we all wrote in our journals. But the whole time I was thinking about going to the park the next day. I had two big worries. The first one was the River Rats. And the second one was my dumb training wheels.

Day 2:

Some of the eggs have hatched. We put thistle leaves in the jar so the caterpillars won't be hungry. They are ugly!

Chapter 5

Part of me wanted to go to the park on Saturday and part of me just wanted to stay home. The chin-up, monkey-bar-swinging part of me wanted to be at the park. The I-am-too-chicken-to-ride-a-two-wheeler part of me wanted to crawl back into bed and pull the covers over my head. By eleven o'clock I decided to go. Better late than never.

I pedalled my bike through the gates of Bayfield Community Park.

Nicholas waved at me right away. "You're finally here!" he shouted. "What took you so long?"

I saw him look at my bike and the training wheels. And even though he didn't say anything, I knew what he was thinking.

Lauren said, "I think the first thing you should do is try to ride *my* bike."

I shook my head.

"Give it a try," she begged. "Nicholas and I will hold it steady. We won't let go. Promise."

And she made an **X** over her heart.

Lauren's bike was really high. The seat was a long way from the ground. I knew if I fell off this bike there would be lots of blood. Probably broken bones. I could even die. I shook my head.

"Pleeease," begged Nicholas. "I know you can do it. Just try."

"Promise you won't let go?" My palms felt sweaty. I really did not want to do this.

Lauren and Nicholas smiled. "We promise!" they said at the same time.

Once I got on, it wasn't as bad as I thought it would be. The bike wobbled back and forth, back and forth. But Lauren and Nicholas kept their promise. They did not let go. Not even once. I could tell that I was getting better at riding. The bike went straight for a longer time. It didn't wobble as much. I was starting to pick up speed.

"That's enough for today." I said. I was out of breath, but I was smiling.

"You'll be riding in no time," said Lauren.

"I knew you could do it," added Nicholas.
"Let's try it again tomorrow."

"Okay," I agreed.

When I got back on my bike, it seemed a
lot smaller. I noticed how low to the ground I
was. My knees were practically touching the
handlebars. We were about to head out of the
park when we heard an unmistakable voice.

"Well, look at what we have here," sneered the voice. "Another baby. This one rides a tricycle."

I had only heard that voice once. But I knew who it was before I saw him — Cameron, the biggest River Rat. My heart sunk like a stone in my chest. This was trouble. I wished I was really brave. Then I'd tell him a thing or two. For starters, *"This isn't a tricycle."* And *"I can almost ride a two-wheeler without the training wheels."* Plus *"I am not a baby."* Except I wasn't brave at all. I stared at Cameron. Oliver and Olivia joined him. I swallowed hard. This was big trouble.

Cameron stared straight at me. "What's your name?" he snarled.

"R-R-Rilla," I stammered.

"Rilla!" laughed Cameron. "What kind of name is that?" He glanced at Oliver and Olivia. He snapped his fingers like he'd just gotten a brilliant idea. "I know! It's an ape name. It's really Rilla *Gorilla*." He turned to Olivia and high-fived her. "Pretty funny, eh?"

"Pretty funny," chimed Olivia. "Rilla Gorilla." She rolled her eyes and snickered.

Oliver started jumping up and down. He pounded his chest and made monkey sounds: *"Ooh ooh ooh."*

"Let's go," said Nicholas. "We're finished here."

You didn't need to tell me twice. I hopped on my bike and pedalled away as fast as I could. From the playground I could hear Cameron yelling, "See you later, Rilla Gorilla!"

"Wait up, Rilla!" Lauren called. She was breathing hard by the time she reached me. "I have an idea." She glanced back toward the playground. "Let's spy on the River Rats."

"Yeah, let's," agreed Nicholas.

I wasn't sure that was a good idea. It would be fun as long as we didn't get caught. But if we did get caught . . . Well, I didn't want to think about it.

We stashed our bikes in the bushes just outside the park and crept over to the gate for a look. They were still at the playground. Cameron was swinging across the monkey bars. He was quick. He reminded me of a monkey swinging from branch to branch. Oliver was flying through the tire run. He was lightning fast. And Olivia was practicing making tight turns on her bike. You could tell she had been riding a two-wheeler for a long time. They were good. Really good. Winning the Fitness Challenge was going to be tough.

Chapter 6

We headed over to Lauren's house for a snack.

"I think we should go back to the park later on," said Nicholas, his mouth full of chocolate chip cookie. "I bet Cameron won't be there then."

Lauren wiped some crumbs off her face. "They'll probably go home for lunch. Maybe we'll have the playground to ourselves."

Just thinking about them gave me butterflies in my stomach. I sighed. "What if they *are* there? They make me nervous."

"Then we won't stay," Lauren promised.

We headed back to the park a little while later. There was no sign of the River Rats. The coast was clear. That icky feeling in my stomach began to disappear. I went straight to the monkey bars. I like the way my hands feel when I swing across. Warm and sweaty. I can even smell the metal on them. Nicholas was jumping through the tire run. Again. And Lauren was trying to do some chin-ups. I could tell by her scrunched-up eyebrows that she was finding it hard to do. I was about halfway across the monkey bars when I heard Cameron's dreaded voice again:

"Rilla Gorilla up a tree,
K - I - S - S - I - N - G,
First comes love,
Then comes marriage,
Then comes …"

I gulped. He was standing right below me. I looked down as his long arms reached up. Then he grabbed hold of my pants and started to pull! I felt my jeans slowly sliding down. He was trying to rip my pants off! In a minute I'd be hanging there in my underwear! I kicked my feet, trying to make him let go, but he held on even tighter. "Stop it!" I screamed.

"Hey, cut it out!" yelled Lauren.

Cameron spun around to face her. "Who's gonna make me? *You*?" He took a step closer to Lauren. Her face turned white.

"Look, Cameron," began Nicholas. "We can all use the park . . ."

"I don't think so," snarled Cameron. "Me and my friends," he pointed to Oliver and Olivia, "we need to practice for the Fitness Challenge. One of us is going to win that new bike. Now beat it!"

I watched Lauren and Nicholas take a step backward. I knew they were scared. I let go of the bar and dropped to the ground. I landed hard, but at least I still had my pants on.

Chapter 7

On Monday morning the first thing I did when I got to school was check on my caterpillars. They had grown a lot. They were very fat. A few of them even had pale yellow stripes. Most of the thistle leaves had been eaten.

Aaron stood next to me. He was staring at his jar. "Rilla," he asked, "what's that in the bottom?"

I took a closer look. Small brown chunks of stuff covered the bottom of the jar. Then I looked at mine, and the other containers. They all had the same brown gunk. Some of them had something that was bigger and wrinkly lying on top of the brown stuff. "I'm not sure," I answered. I turned toward Claire. "Do you know what it is?"

Claire peered into the jar. "Just a sec," she said. She pulled a magnifying glass out of her back pocket. When she saw the surprised look on my face, she said, "I thought this might come in handy today. I brought it from my detective kit at home." Leave it to Claire. She is so smart. She always plans ahead.

"Well, I'm not sure about all that brown stuff." She paused. "It kind of reminds me of cookie crumbs. But I think that wrinkly thing is the caterpillar's old skin. I'm pretty sure they've started to molt."

"Let me see." I grabbed the magnifying glass from Claire. The old skin was really thin. I could practically see through it. "Cool!" I said.

"And look," added Aaron. "There's more skins here. And here. And here." He pointed to the rest of the jars.

Ms MacArthur joined us. "You all seem pretty excited. What's going on?"

I held up my jar for her to see. "The caterpillars are molting," I answered. "Look at the old skins on the bottom."

Ms MacArthur took the magnifying glass. She studied the skins for a long time. "The larvae are really changing, aren't they? Don't forget to add some new thistle leaves. These little guys are always eating. Right now it's really important that they have plenty of food."

"Okay," I said, "but we can't figure something out." I pointed to the jar. "What's that crumbly brown stuff?"

The teacher laughed. "Butterfly droppings," she answered.

"Droppings?" asked Aaron. He looked puzzled.

I nudged him with my elbow. "Poop!" I laughed. "It's poop."

"*Eeew*, gross," he said, wrinkling up his face.

"So much for it looking like cookie crumbs," I laughed. "The jar is filled with poop. Oops," I added, "I mean butterfly droppings."

Aaron got this funny look on his face. He does that whenever he's getting a good idea. "You know," he whispered so Ms MacArthur wouldn't hear, "the droppings could come in handy."

"What do you mean?" I whispered back.

He looked at the teacher and then he lowered his voice even more. "We could use the poop to get even with the River Rats. Put it in their sneakers or make poop-sicles." He laughed.

I laughed, too. "That would be so much fun.

Maybe we could . . ." But before I could finish, I heard Ms MacArthur tell everyone it was time for gym. That's my most favorite thing at school. Sometimes we ride scooters. Sometimes we do gymnastics. Sometimes we play games. Today we were still practicing for the Fitness Challenge.

Mr. Kempton, the gym teacher, already had everything set up when we arrived. There were long ropes to climb. Bars to do chin-ups. Hoops to race through. All kinds of stuff.

"Good morning boys and girls," boomed Mr. Kempton's voice. "Today we'll continue practicing for the Bayfield Fitness Challenge. I know every one of you would like to win that X-Treme bike. But it's not really about winning a bike. It's about being physically fit. It's about being active and staying healthy." He smiled at all of us. "So break into your squads and head to a station."

I'm in the same squad as Tony, James and Bethany. It was our turn to start at the chin-ups station. James went first. He did two chin-ups. Then it was Bethany's turn. She finds it really hard. She only did one. I said I'd go last. I wanted to see if I could beat Tony. He is really good at doing chin-ups. Last gym day he did three. Today he beat his old score and did five. Now it was my turn. I gripped the wooden bar with two hands and pulled myself up. Up. Down. I could hear Tony counting. I knew he wanted to do more than me.

"Three, four."

The muscles in my arms started to shake.

"Fiiiiiiive."

My face felt hot and sweaty. I could barely pull myself up. But I needed to do just one more to beat Tony.

"Six . . ." he counted out loud. "Seven . . ."

I dropped to the floor. Seven! I beat Tony by two! And he is the best in our class.

"You got me, Rilla," said Tony. "But wait till next time." He grinned. "I'll probably do *twenty*."

I grinned. "We'll see," I answered. So now I knew if I kept practicing, I'd be able to do

the most chin-ups. But that didn't help me with the bicycle obstacle course. How was I ever going to drive around a bunch of cones without knocking them over? And the worst part was, I had to somehow do it without my training wheels.

Chapter 8

When we got back to our room it was time for our Morning Meeting. I remembered that Claire was supposed to have a riddle for the class today. I knew it would be a good one.

Ms MacArthur smiled at us as we entered the classroom. "By the looks on your faces, I think you all had a lot of fun in gym today," she said. "I hope we have as much fun in the classroom. Let's start with our Morning Meeting and Claire's riddle."

Claire smiled. "It's a tough one. I bet no one will be able to guess the answer."

Once everyone was sitting on the story carpet, Ms MacArthur gave us the day's instructions. Then it was time for Claire's riddle. "What has antlers and sucks blood?" she asked.

"A hungry deer?" guessed Kris.

"Nope."

"Dracula?" guessed Jenn.

"Nope," answered Claire. "It's . . ." she paused and looked at all of us, ". . . a *moose-quito!*" Then she laughed. "Get it?"

I laughed. So did the other kids. I can hardly ever guess the answers to riddles.

Ms MacArthur interrupted my thoughts. "Boys and girls, now it's time to check on your larvae. And remember to record any changes in your Life Cycle Journal."

I got my caterpillar jar and sat down at a table. Nicholas was next to me. He was already busy writing in his journal. He stopped and looked over at me. "Do you want to go to the park after school and do some practicing?" he asked.

I thought about the park and all the fun we could have using the equipment. I thought about winning the new X-Treme bike. Then I thought about the River Rats. They would ruin everything. The last time had been way too scary. I shook my head. "I don't want to go back to the park," I whispered. I didn't look at Nicholas but I could feel him staring at me. I pretended to be really interested in my caterpillar jar.

"You're a scaredy-cat," Nicholas replied.

"Am not!" I hissed back.

"Are so!"

"Am *not*!"

"Good," grinned Nicholas. "Then you can meet me in the park right after school."

So it was settled. I didn't really want to go

to the park. But I didn't really want to stay home either. One thing was for sure — I definitely did not want to run into the River Rats again.

I picked up my jar and then I wrote in my journal.

Day 5:

The caterpillars are getting fat. Some are climbing the sides of the jar. A few have shed their skin. There is something that looks like threads in the jar.

Before I knew it, the day was over. It was bus time.

"See you at the park," called Lauren, as I boarded the bus. I had that sinking feeling in the pit of my stomach. It's the kind of feeling you get when you want to do something, yet you don't want to do something. I sure hoped things would work out okay.

* * *

I arrived at Bayfield Community Park right

on time. Lauren and Nicholas were exactly where they'd promised they'd be — by the main gates. As soon as I got there, I noticed they looked worried.

"Were you afraid I wasn't coming?" I teased.

"No," answered Lauren. "Look." She pointed toward the swings. It was the River Rats. They were using the playground equipment.

My mouth went dry. I found it hard to swallow. My belly started doing flip-flops. "Let's get out of here," I whispered.

Nicholas shook his head. "No, we can't let a bunch of bullies ruin our time. We'll stick together. There are three of them and three of us."

"We'll ignore them," said Lauren, but she looked worried. "Rilla, we all need to train. This is the only place to practice. Please stay," she begged.

I did not want to stay. But Nicholas was right. We couldn't let the River Rats ruin our time. And if we stuck together, maybe nothing would happen. Besides, I had a surprise for Lauren and Nicholas. All weekend I had practiced riding my brother's bigger bike. I could ride without training wheels. Not well, but maybe well enough.

"Okay," I agreed. "I'll stay. But we stick together. Deal?" Even as I said it, the memory of Cameron trying to pull down my pants made me shiver.

"I'll set up some rocks," said Nicholas. "We can pretend they're cones. That way we can get lots of practice."

We took turns weaving in and around the rocks. I used Lauren's bike since mine still had the training wheels on. At first I was pretty wobbly. I concentrated hard. In. Out. In. Out. I was doing it! I wasn't fast but I was getting better. I kept one eye on the rock cones and the other eye on Cameron, Olivia and Oliver. They had stopped playing on the swings and were watching us. I tried to ignore them but it wasn't easy. Around one rock, around another. One more to go and . . . *uh oh* . . .

Suddenly Cameron was standing right in front of me. How did that happen? He had his hands behind his back, an evil smile on his face. This was trouble with a capital T. Before I knew what was happening, he whipped out a stick and shoved it through the spokes of my front wheel. The bike pitched forward. I flew over the handlebars and landed on the pavement with a big thud. For a moment I

couldn't breathe. I felt like all the air had been knocked out of me. Then everything started to hurt at once. My stomach hurt. My elbows hurt. My hands were scraped. Blood oozed from my knees. Tears burned my eyes.

"Are you all right, Rilla?" asked Lauren. She bent down and helped me up off the pavement.

"Sorry, Lauren. Hope your bike's okay."

Nicholas glared at Cameron. "Leave us alone!" he shouted. "We're not bothering you." It was like everything had been bottled up inside him. It all came pouring out at once. "Why'd you do that? You're always picking on us. You're nothing but a bully. Now leave us alone."

For a moment there was total silence. I'm not sure who was more surprised — Cameron or Nicholas. Cameron just stood there, staring at Nicholas, his mouth hanging open. Nicholas clenched and unclenched his fists. Finally Cameron muttered something that sounded like "little babies" and hurried back to Oliver and Olivia.

Chapter 9

After that, we headed over to Lauren's house. I couldn't decide what hurt more — my scraped hands, my bloody knees or my feelings. It took half a box of Band-Aids to cover all the cuts, plus four double fudge brownies and a big glass of milk before I started to feel better. No one said a word while we ate, but I knew that Lauren and Nicholas were thinking exactly what I was thinking. We needed to practice in the park. The Fitness Challenge was in two weeks. But none of us wanted to run into the River Rats again. Ever.

"Maybe we should take a break," suggested Nicholas. He looked down at my torn pants. You could see the Band-Aids through the holes. "Just for today," he added.

"I think that's a good idea," said Lauren. "We could try going back tomorrow. What do you think, Rilla?"

That was the last thing I wanted to do. Part of me just wanted to give up. Another part of me wanted to show those River Rats that we could beat them in the Fitness Challenge. One of *us* could win the X-Treme bicycle. And the helmet. And the water bottle. "Maybe . . ." I answered.

Lauren smiled at me. "How about we hunt for butterflies? We could bring them in to show Ms MacArthur tomorrow."

"That would be cool," agreed Nicholas. "Who knows, maybe we'll even find a Painted Lady."

We hunted everywhere for butterflies. We even searched for thistles because we had learned that Painted Ladies love to eat the leaves. But, so far, our jar only had two ladybugs and three very fluffy caterpillars. The caterpillars didn't look at all like the ugly ones we had at school. These were fat and furry. Kind of cute. When I touched one, it curled into a tight ball.

Eventually we gave up on finding any butterflies and started back for Lauren's. We headed past the park and that's when I saw something interesting. Cameron was still there — alone. There was no sign of Oliver or Olivia. One mean River Rat, all by himself.

"Hey, look over there," I said. I pointed to Cameron. "Looks like he has a problem." Cameron was trying to wiggle through a large plastic tube. His head was poking out one end. His feet were poking out the other. But his shoulders weren't moving at all. His face was red and sweaty.

Nicholas stopped to watch. "I think he's stuck," he said.

"He *is* stuck," said Lauren. She laughed. "Serves him right. That big bully deserves to stay there forever. Let's see how long it takes for him to get out."

"I have a better idea," I said. "Watch this." I grabbed the jar from Nicholas and carefully removed the fattest caterpillar.

"What are you going to do?" asked Lauren.

I looked down at my torn pants. Then I looked at Lauren. "It's payback time."

"Are you crazy?" she gasped.

But I didn't answer her. Before I lost my nerve, I marched across the park and stood face to face with Cameron. He couldn't hurt me now. "Having a problem?" I asked in my sweetest voice. "Maybe this will help." And I gently placed the caterpillar on his nose.

Cameron's eyes bulged. He twitched his nose. He bobbed his head wildly, trying to shake off the caterpillar. "Get it off my face!" he screamed. "Get it off!"

The caterpillar inched its way down his nose and headed toward his mouth. "That's for the bloody knees you gave me today. And for these." I held up my bandaged hands. Cameron shook his head even harder, but that furry little caterpillar stuck to him like glue. "I hear caterpillars taste delicious," I said, and then I turned and ran back to Lauren and Nicholas.

I could hear Cameron screaming, "I'll get you for this! I'll get you for this! You'll be sorry!"

* * *

"Did you see the look on Cameron's face?" I asked, once we were back at Lauren's house. "I got him good!"

"I wonder how caterpillars taste," Nicholas said, laughing. "Squish them up for soup. Bake them in your favorite muffins. Sprinkle them on your cereal." He was really getting into this.

But Lauren sat quietly on the floor. She wasn't saying a word. She was arranging and rearranging her teddy bear collection.

"Wasn't that just too funny?" I asked Lauren.

Lauren stared at me, her eyes big and round. "I'm not sure that was such a good thing to do," she finally answered. "It was funny," she went on, "but what will happen next time we go to the park? What if Cameron swallows the caterpillar?"

Suddenly the room was quiet. No one said a word. What had I been thinking? Cameron would definitely get even. Today had been bad enough. I had the bloody knees and scraped hands to prove it. I couldn't even begin to imagine what he would do the next time he saw me. "Maybe we should go back and check on him. Make sure he's still not stuck," I said. I crossed my fingers. "With any luck, he didn't eat that caterpillar."

But when we got to the park there was no sign of Cameron. He was gone. I wasn't sure if that was a good thing or a bad thing.

Chapter 10

The next day, I woke up with a plan. As soon as I got to school I talked to my friends about it. The plan was this: whenever I went to the park, I would go with a whole bunch of kids. Kind of like my own gang. Then there would be no more worries about the River Rats.

Everyone thought it was a great idea. So, after school today, there will be a new gang at the park — all Bayfield kids. Maybe we'll even give ourselves a name. Something cool like the Bayfield Bullets. James, Claire, Aaron, Tony and Matthew would meet Lauren, me and Nicholas. And we would stick together. I've heard my mom say that there's safety in numbers. I hope it's true.

The next thing I did was check on my

caterpillars. I couldn't believe what I saw. Almost every one was hanging from the top of the jar in the shape of a hook. Kind of like a J.

"Wow," I said to Claire. "Look at that. Your caterpillars are doing the same thing as mine."

Claire studied her jar. Of course she whipped out her magnifying glass again. That girl is always prepared. Then she said, "Take a look, Rilla. This one looks different from the rest."

I peered into her jar. Sure enough, one caterpillar was totally wrapped in white threads. "I think it's making a chrysalis," I said.

I wrote in my journal:

Day 6:
Almost every caterpillar looks like a J. One of them has formed a chrysalis. It must be really hard work because the caterpillar is wiggling back and forth like crazy.

The day seemed really long. Math was hard. Our spelling words were tricky. Gym was actually boring. All I could think about was the River Rats. What would Cameron do to get even? And he *would* get even. Would he beat me up? Try to pull down my pants again? Make me eat dirt? Just thinking about it gave me a pain in my stomach.

At bus time, Tony gave me a thumbs-up signal. "See you at the park, Rilla. We'll show those River Rats who's boss."

"I guess," I mumbled. But I had a bad feeling about it.

* * *

At exactly four o'clock we met at the gates. There were eight of us altogether: Tony, Lauren, James, Claire, Aaron, Nicholas, Matthew and, of course, me. I led the way. And I have to admit that it felt good. For once I felt like I was in charge. That worried feeling had almost disappeared. But a teeny voice in my head was screaming, *"You're crazy, crazy, crazy!"*

We rode our bikes straight to the monkey bars. Of course, Cameron, Oliver and Olivia were already there. Cameron jumped down when he saw us. "Get lost, Rilla Gorilla!"

I took a deep breath and before I could chicken out, I said in a loud voice, "We need to use the equipment, too. There's enough room for everyone here."

Cameron's eyes widened. He stared at me. Then at all eight of us. I folded my arms across my chest and stared right back. He looked a bit stunned. I wasn't sure if it was because of the way I was acting or the sight of so many Bayfield kids.

He looked over at Oliver and Olivia and shrugged his shoulders. Finally he spoke. "Let's get out of here. We got better things to do."

I watched as the River Rats hopped on their bicycles and rode off. I didn't realize that my heart was pounding until they were out of sight. I took a deep breath and slowly let it out. That felt good. I had taken charge.

Nicholas grinned at me. "Way to go, Rilla. You showed them."

Chapter 11

For the rest of the week we met at the park after school. I was feeling good about two things. First, I felt a lot safer being there with a bunch of kids. The River Rats seemed to have vanished and we pretty much had the park to ourselves. I bet they were still practicing but probably somewhere else. Second, I was feeling really good about the competition. I was improving in everything, including the bicycle obstacle course. My training wheels were off, and there was just one week left until the Fitness Challenge.

Things had even gotten better at school. We were doing fun stuff in math. I aced my spelling quiz and in gym we were learning how to play basketball. But the best part was the butterfly project. Nearly all the caterpillars had spun chrysalises. And I knew it wouldn't be long before the first butterfly hatched.

In my best printing I wrote in my journal:

> **Day 9:**
> The chrysalis has changed color. It is sort of green. There are silver and gold dots on it.

Claire was drawing a picture in her journal. She stopped coloring. "We don't have many more days to practice," she said. "The competition is the end of next week. Who do you think will win?"

I shrugged my shoulders. I knew it would be close. It seemed like each of the Bayfield kids was an expert at something. James was the best at swinging across the monkey bars. Aaron was the best at the tire run. And no one could beat Lauren on a bicycle. Anybody could win. "I guess it will depend on how the judges score the points." I paused. "I'd love to win that bike. Then I'd be rid of my little bike for good. But, you know, I don't really care who wins, as long as it's not a River Rat."

Claire nodded her head. She understood exactly what I meant.

Ms MacArthur stopped at our table. She looked at my journal first. "You have some nice details in your pictures, Rilla," she said. "I especially like how you showed the chrysalis attached to the silk button." Claire's was next. Ms MacArthur looked puzzled. "What's this part, Claire?" She pointed to a small glued flap.

Claire laughed. "Lift it and see."

"Leave it to you, Claire. Of course, you'd add a butterfly riddle!" Ms MacArthur read the riddle. "Why did the boy throw the butter out the window?" She smiled. "I remember that riddle from when I was a little kid."

I could tell Claire was surprised about that. "Really?" she asked. "So what's the answer? Why did the boy throw the butter out the window?"

"He wanted to see the butter fly," replied Ms MacArthur with a laugh.

Claire grinned. "I'll have to get a trickier one next time."

* * *

I couldn't believe how fast the next week went. One day the Bayfield Fitness Challenge was five days away, and BOOM!, just like that, it was Friday, the day before the competition. Everything was happening so fast. Today was the last day to practice at the park. All the kids were going to be there — Lauren, Tony, Aaron, Nicholas, Bethany — everybody. We all wanted to win the X-Treme bike. But there could be only one winner. I crossed my fingers. Maybe, just maybe, it would be me.

I was the last one to arrive at the playground. I couldn't believe how many kids were there. The place was really crowded. All the equipment was being used. The good news was that everyone who was practicing was doing their very best. Nicholas was racing through the tire run. He was getting a lot faster. Aaron was working on his chin-ups. But he still wasn't very good at it. And Lauren was riding her bike around some rock cones she had set up. I couldn't believe how speedy she was. She didn't wobble at all. Not even once. The bad news was that the River Rats were there. But they didn't seem to be bothering anybody. They were using the monkey bars.

"Hi, Rilla!" Lauren shouted. She waved me over. "Check this out!" She pedalled in and around the rocks again, making tight turns. "Pretty good, eh?"

"That's great! I bet you'll win the competition. Nobody can do that better than you." I glanced toward the monkey bars. I lowered my voice. "I see we've got company." I nodded in the direction of Cameron, Olivia and Oliver.

"I'm not going to let them wreck my day. Let's just ignore them," suggested Lauren. "They won't do anything to us. There are too many other kids here."

I sure hoped she was right. I watched Cameron swing across the monkey bars, drop to the ground and then head off to use another piece of equipment. Oliver followed — across the bars, down to the ground and off to the swings. *Monkey see, monkey do*, I thought. Then Olivia started. She got about halfway across when suddenly she lost her grip. She screamed and fell to the ground. Hard. She lay there not moving.

I didn't think about her being a River Rat. I didn't think about Cameron and how mean he was to me. I didn't think about much of anything. Everything happened at top speed. I dropped my bike and tore across the playground. I knelt down beside Olivia. Her face was white and her brown eyes looked extra big. "Are you okay?" I asked.

Olivia stared at me and slowly nodded. I could tell by the look on her face that she was surprised to see me kneeling beside her. I grabbed her hand and slowly pulled her to her feet. "Thanks," she said, and she seemed to be all right.

"Sis!" Oliver came scrambling as fast as he could across the grass and stopped next to me. He didn't say anything. He was panting, trying to catch his breath. He just stood there staring at Olivia, until his breathing returned to normal.

"Did you hurt yourself?" he asked her.

"I'm fine, Ollie. Really," answered Olivia. "My hands slipped, but I'm okay. *Oww*," she moaned, "my butt's sore." She rubbed her hand over her rear end.

Oliver turned and faced me. Here it comes. Will he call me Rilla Gorilla? Tell me to mind my own business? Or maybe he'll give me a shove and tell me to get lost. Then, very softly, he said one word I never expected to hear: "Thanks."

Chapter 12

The day of the Bayfield Community Fitness Challenge was finally here. It wasn't too hot and it wasn't too cold. It was a perfect day. I was feeling good about the competition. I knew I could race through the tire run in record speed. I could swing across the monkey bars just about as quick as James. I didn't think anything else would be a problem — except for the bicycle obstacle course. Just thinking about it made me think about that new X-Treme bicycle. Boy, it sure would be sweet to win that.

I arrived at the park at exactly 9:45. The competition would start in just fifteen minutes. The first person I saw was Claire. She was so excited she was practically vibrating all over. "I can't believe it's today," she said. "I've been awake forever. Who do you think will win?" Before I could open my mouth, she blurted out, "Look! There's James and Aaron. Oh! And Lauren and Tony!" She was talking extra fast. "Let's go see them." I didn't have time to answer her. She hopped on her bike and pedalled off in their direction.

"Wait for me!" I hollered.

A few minutes later an announcement boomed out through a megaphone, "Would all contestants for the Bayfield Fitness Challenge please meet at the tire run? The competition is about to begin."

Everyone gathered at the tire run, and I mean everyone. Cameron, Olivia and Oliver were there, plus a whole pile of kids I didn't even know. We all had to line up for score cards. Then a tall man with a moustache held up his hand for quiet.

"Welcome, boys and girls, to the First Annual Bayfield Fitness Challenge. Today's events promise to be lots of fun. We have some awesome prizes," he said, and he pointed to a green X-Treme bike. It had a really cool-looking helmet and a silver water bottle. "Now, here's how the challenge works. For each event you compete in, you will score points. These will be added together and the person with the most points in total wins the competition. Pretty easy, right?"

I looked around at all the kids. Some were nodding. Others were staring at the bicycle.

"Let's get started," continued the man. "The first event is the tire run."

Aaron raced through those tires like he was being chased by a mad dog. He won that event — no problem. We collected our points and we headed to the monkey bars. James practically flew across the bars and beat his old time easily. Then it was off to do some

76

chin-ups. I was pumped when I did nine. That was more than Tony, more than anyone so far. I watched Cameron try to beat me. He was up to six. Then his face got all red and sweaty.

He grunted and dropped to the ground. *Yes!* I beat him. That made me feel great.

So far, I had thirty-seven points altogether. James thrust his score card at me. "Check out how many points I have." He was practically beaming. He had the next best Bayfield score — thirty-two.

"That's awesome, James," I said. "Isn't this so much fun?"

But James didn't answer me. Instead he nudged me. "Look who's here."

The River Rats were standing right in front of me. All three of them. Cameron leaned down close to my face. I could tell he'd had some peanut butter for breakfast. A brown gob was on his chin. It made me think of caterpillar droppings. I smiled at that. "What are you smiling at, Rilla Gorilla?" he snapped. Before I knew what was happening, he grabbed my score card. "Bet I have more points than you," he said.

"Give that back to me," I yelled, but Cameron hid it behind his back.

"Make me," he taunted. He held the card high above his head.

I jumped to grab it but his arms were just too long. He squinted at the scores. Then he frowned. "What?" he bellowed. "You have thirty-seven points? That's impossible. I have thirty-six and I'm *waaaaaaay* better than you."

Lauren, Aaron and James inched closer to me. Cameron tossed my card back but he flashed me a nasty grin. "There's only one more challenge, Rilla Gorilla — the bicycle obstacle course. Guess you can kiss that new bike goodbye. It'll be mine."

For a minute it felt like there was a big stone in my chest, instead of my heart. This was a good-bad situation. Being in first place was good — even though I was practically tied with a big bully. But it was bad that it all came down to the bicycle obstacle course. I had practiced riding Lauren's bike every day. And then my own bike, with the training wheels off. I would be using my own bike today. But there was no way I could beat Cameron. I had seen him ride around the rock cones without ever touching one. He was fast and he was good.

I watched a lot of kids go through the course. Then it was Lauren's turn. She was amazing! She got ten points! The judges began announcing the updated scores. I crossed my fingers. Lauren hadn't done as well in the other events, so I was still in the lead for total points — with Cameron just behind.

Then it was my turn to ride through the course. I took a deep breath and let it out slowly. Could I navigate around all ten cones without knocking any of them down?

Chapter 13

Focus. *I can do this*, I said to myself, and I pushed down with my right foot. My left knee grazed the handlebar. Around the first orange cone. Around the second cone. Focus. I felt my bike wobble. Oh no! I barely made it around the third one. Out of the corner of my eye, I saw the cone teeter back and forth. *Please don't let it fall over.* Down it went! My bike kept wobbling. *I can do this*, I thought. The fourth cone fell over. Now there was no way I could win the competition. I was sure Cameron wouldn't knock down *any* cones. Tears came to my eyes. All of my hard work was for nothing. Right then and there I felt like quitting. That was until I saw Cameron watching me. He was smirking. It was like he

already knew he had won the X-Treme bike. And that made me mad. I pedalled harder, a little faster. My bike seemed steadier. Around the other cones. I didn't knock over any more and that meant I had gained a total of eight points. My final score was forty-five. Now it was Cameron's turn.

Cameron only needed nine points to win. That would be a cinch for him. I was pretty sure he could ride his bike blindfolded and not knock over any cones. He stared at the obstacle course. I could tell he was really concentrating. He didn't look at any of the spectators. Then he started pedalling. Around one cone. Around two cones. Three. Four. Five. Six. He was up to the seventh cone. There was no way he'd lose. He cruised past me. My heart sank as he approached the finish line. I was toast.

The eighth cone loomed closer. As Cameron whipped around it, he looked back and grinned. He stuck out his tongue and wiggled it at me. But that was a big mistake. By the time he turned around, he was practically on top of the ninth cone. He swerved hard to get around it. Too late! The cone toppled over. Cameron struggled to gain control of his bike. He steered to the left, then to the right. Now he was on top of the tenth cone. The bike skidded and he drove right over it!

That meant he only earned eight points. I had won!

My heart was pounding. I jumped up and down. "Woo hoo!" I shouted.

Lauren smiled. "Way to go, Rilla. You deserve to win."

"That's what he gets for being such a show-off," added Nicholas, nodding in Cameron's direction.

I looked over at Cameron. He was definitely not happy. He jumped off his bike and threw it to the ground. Then he stomped off toward Olivia and Oliver.

"Poor sport," muttered Nicholas.

I thought about all the trouble Cameron had caused — bossing the Bayfield kids around, calling me names, trying to pull down my pants. I remembered my bloody knees and skinned hands. Part of me felt a teeny bit sorry for him for acting so stupid during the obstacle course. He really *was* better at it than I was. But the rest of me was just too excited. I had won the Fitness Challenge with lots of hard work, fair and square. It would be totally awesome riding that X-Treme bike with my friends.

Lauren nudged me. She had the biggest grin on her face. She pointed to the man with the megaphone. He was standing next to the coolest-looking bike in the whole wide world. Then he announced for all to hear, "And the winner of the First Annual Bayfield Fitness Challenge is . . . Marilla Wilson!"

Chapter 14

On Monday I wanted to ride my new X-Treme bike to school, but it was too far to go. So I took the bus like I do every day. One thing was for sure: I knew what I would be doing the minute I got home — riding my brand new X-Treme bike!

As soon as I walked into the classroom I knew something was up. Ms MacArthur looked frazzled. That was weird. She never gets frazzled. In fact, everybody seemed really excited. A whole bunch of kids were over by the windows. They were all talking at once.

"Here's one!"

"Here's another one!"

"There are five over here!"

I looked at Ms MacArthur. "What's going on?" I asked, still standing in the doorway.

She looked really panicked. "Quick! Close the door, Rilla. Don't let any out!"

"Let what out?" I asked.

"The butterflies," she moaned. "They all hatched over the weekend and now they're loose in the classroom. Most of them are on the windowsills, but be careful where you walk. They're everywhere."

"Hey, Rilla, get back here!" hollered Lauren. "We need your help."

I watched as Lauren very gently scooped a Painted Lady off the windowsill and placed it in a cardboard box covered with fine netting. "Now, watch this," she said. She picked up another butterfly and held out her hand. The butterfly sat there, slowly pumping its wings. "Isn't it awesome?"

It took us almost till recess time to catch all the butterflies.

"Well, boys and girls," began Ms MacArthur, "I think our science project was a huge success. Altogether we have a total of forty-five Painted Ladies. We'll release our butterflies in Bayfield Woods after recess."

Aaron looked over at me. "Forty-five butterflies," he repeated. "Wasn't that your score on the Fitness Challenge?"

I nodded my head.

"Hey, congratulations on winning the competition," he said. Then he laughed. "Guess you'll never forget that number."

"Never," I agreed.

* * *

Releasing the butterflies was amazing. At first, only a couple of them flew out of the box. It was as if they didn't want to leave us. Then gradually, one by one, they spread their wings and were gone. I stood very still as a Painted Lady flew around my head. Then it fluttered over and landed very gently on Lauren's cheek. I laughed out loud. It reminded me of the time I put the caterpillar on Cameron's face. Only this was way better.

The butterflies flitted from plant to plant. Some flew so far that they totally disappeared. The ones that stayed behind just seemed to know where to find the thistles. In and out, up and around they flew. It was like they were competing in their own obstacle course. The reward this time wouldn't be a new bicycle and it wouldn't be for just one kid. It would be something that all of the Bayfield kids could enjoy. I was pretty sure that soon there would be lots of eggs on those plants. We'd be welcoming a whole new family of Painted Lady butterflies.